A GERMAN
PICTURESQUE

A German Picturesque

JASON SCHWARTZ

ALFRED A. KNOPF   NEW YORK   1998

THIS IS A BORZOI BOOK
PUBLISHED BY ALFRED A. KNOPF, INC.

www.randomhouse.com

Portions of this book first appeared in *Conjunctions, Exact Change
Yearbook, The Quarterly,* and *StoryQuarterly.*

Library of Congress Cataloging-in-Publication Data
Schwartz, Jason.
A German picturesque / by Jason Schwartz.
p.   cm.
ISBN 0-679-44332-0
I. Title.
PS3569.C56579G47 1998
813'.54—dc21   97-50555   CIP

Manufactured in the United States of America
First Edition

FOR JEREMY SCHWARTZ
(1970–1992)

CONTENTS

I

He tends to his correspondence. Millicent, for instance, in France. Mother dear. He opens the doors of the armoire. He plays symphonies and minuets on the gramophone. He reads about Cinna, about Agrippa, about towns in America. He reads about birds. He counts hours.

He weeps.

Let me describe this.

The wind blows at the windows. There is a mirror hanging above the nightstand. There are figurines arranged on the mantel.

The clock ticks black.

They mention a ship sunk in the Atlantic.

A postage stamp exhibits a king's profile, the ruff green, it seems, the crown a bit askew, but grim, also—and terrifying, I have always thought. His carriage was stopped in the countryside and the party was slaughtered—the queen wearing a string of pearls, a steward carrying a parcel of chocolate. The epigraph, in Gothic, refers to squirrels and to the dogtooth along the road—but appears here, according to the philatelists, by accident.

An address is lost.

They mention partridgeberry, pudding, a mosquito. They mention flowers—but which flowers? And what of the stems? And what of the colors? Simply a fellow's clumsy little gift, bunched, yes, and pleasant, but nevertheless wrong, certainly, given the curtains, given the light. They mention birds—something about the feathers, the warmth of the feathers, perhaps something about the softness of them, plumes and vanes, simply a wren, finally, or even a swallow, that the woman still remembers. They mention another family, too—and how, after all, she had loved a certain other fellow (witness, though, the wife's clean apron, the fresh tobacco on a tray)—and how, moreover, the father and mother had been found in the water off Claw (in just the fashion one would imagine).

She does not mention the town in Spain, the lavender tabletop, the tiny porcelain swan.

Meadow rue, or *Thalictrum aquilegifolium*, grew—famously—in Lambeth Borough, beneath, indeed, the steward's window. King Edward adored sweet William, or *Dianthus barbatus,* and buttercup, or *Ranunculus,* of the creeping sort. A framed rendering of Miss Lingard, or *Phlox glaberrina,* which was beloved, which was kept in the woman's bureau, burned in a great fire in 1926.

He fusses over the baggage—keys and such, creases. He admires the doors of the armoire, the figures carved into the bureau, various items on the mantel. He looks at pictures in a picture book. For instance: a prince dancing a waltz. Maidens bathing in a lake. Beggar's-lice and azaleas near a graveyard.

A bug crawls across the tabletop.

There are pennies, a gramophone.

He eats tripe. He stokes the fire. He goes from room to room.

He trembles.

The wind blows at the windows. There are saucers, crumbs on a platter, sassafras.

There is a shining spot on the doorknob.

Caesar's brother, or *Iris sibirica,* which is sometimes poisonous, and Mrs. Bradshaw, or *Geum chiloense,* which grew near the garden urn, were covered with mud. King Edward died—elegantly, apparently—in a patch of dogtooth, or *Erythronium*. Needlepoint, or *Hedera helix,* grew outside an orphanage, where, somebody had said, all the children stammered, and had hives, and were knock-kneed. Crowberry, or *Empetrum nigrum,* grew in Worms, but the rockery and the house were ruined during the war, and everybody moved away.

He mentions fugues, thundershowers, alpaca.

He forgets most of the names, most of the dates, and, further, Cornelia is referred to only at the end, which is sad, quite possibly—something about the clouds, perhaps, or a shadow on the grass, a flagon (if I have the correct term) that cracked in two. But how is one to gloss this? His wife had admired Cinna, for instance, and now, here, see the book upon the tabletop. Does this settle the matter? Well, there is symmetry, evidently—or, anyway, this is what they say. There is a reference, moreover, to Agrippa's reflection in a pond, but this is not something I would ever have noticed—no. Nor, indeed, am I even certain what is implied, exactly. Please tell me—is the book shut? Is the room warm? Is the man still?

He mentions his mother's scarf, to begin with,

and the pinafore his brother had worn for an automobile ride, la la la la, a Sunday afternoon in June. He mentions his mother's petunias, too, and the nightshade, and the trampled Joan Wilcox, which he finds affecting—something about the month, I suppose, or the way she would smooth her sleeves.

Let me rephrase this.

A letter is lost.

A postage stamp exhibits an emblem, a portrait and a shield, and a buggy in town—barber, bank, five and dime, orphanage. The funeral parlor is farther off, and bright, bright, it seems, the lamps at the steps—though the windows are fogged over, and the entablature, rather curiously, always reminds me of the figurines arranged on the mantel. Finally, little nudes appear next to the name (should we know which?) and above the dates.

Permit me an aside.

Aunt Estelle was married in August: birch trees, marble pillars, a lawn. Aunt Mae cried for her father: Aunt Blanche came alone. Aunt Audrey brought a candy dish, but it broke in the box. A child in a bow tie played the piano and sang: Antwerp, tea cake, a hat. Aunt Estelle was married in August, but the groom was poor. Aunt Harriet had polio: Aunt Blanche came alone.

She stands on the porch. She wears a bonnet. Her suitcases are all about. She waits, you see. Is there something tender here?—the rain, say, or the winter, or the way she holds her hands?

There is a carton with gloves and pincushions, charms, a rag doll—but her mother's goblet was left behind, my, my—or, anyway, it cannot be found, which is a great disappointment, certainly. What will become of such a thing? It suggests the vase, I think, and the boy alone at supper—though, no, perhaps this is not apt, actually.

The trunk, somebody had said, is the color of peaches out of season.

He plays an opera on the gramophone. He reads about Caesar, about Caesar's brother, about the Barons' War.

There were robins and crowberry one summer.

There are saucers, a plate, a spoon, molasses. There is a globe. There is a white box tied with red ribbon.

There is no mail.

He reads about the Comtesse du Barry, about muskets, about the watermark. He writes out the days of the week, the months of the year. He turns pages. He is mistaken.

He draws the blinds.

A bug crawls across the tabletop.

THE AUNT

This was the first one. So, you must understand, there was harm, after all—oh, yes, and all the fuss, and this bit of hair in the cold, crooked and worn, dear me, curled this way when she was ill.

The crepe was kept—it is not yet hopeless!—and part of the shirt was moist, though the cuff was stiff about the ends—though the strip was bent and left, too. Oh, my, but how the rest is bunched and precious: their hands were at the collar.

But certainly he looked—now here was some of his mother's sash—fine: like, that is to say, her husband, or, if you would prefer—more simply—his father. It is so sad, this row! It is hopeless—though she wore her mother's gown—a cur, she said—snug here, a piece, you see, held: but here, unhappily, it was black.

The orchestra played in the garden.

Well, yes—eventually. Please understand there was only a gesture. Oh, the question, presumably, of the wrinkle, the cackle, the Danube. (Loss—of a sort.) They never came for the summer.

The flowers were worn in just this manner—or, if you like, as his had been. There were fewer, indeed, every time. These, clearly, were from Derbe—though they were tangled, though they were not pinned properly.

Well, the noise and wane in the aisle that day. A mole, you will recall. A stake, mumped, in the quack grass, in the neat square, in the tier of flowers: his were amiss. A ringlet of his hair moved handsomely (and nobody saw).

THE DAUGHTER

The trunk was purchased by her family. The brass handles at the sides looked—her mother said—like a queen's bosoms. A pox! (They did not go away on holiday anymore.) The wood was scraped next to the wire and across the nice curlicues in their names—hers first.

Their last name was—the bride said—homely. The chiffonier, nevertheless—but, nevertheless, the ruffle and the peach pit (prattle, merely). Was she standing in this fashion? Well, it is only such a tiny thing—but in any case.

It was because she was terribly sweet—or rather, actually, because it was a pity. He touched her wrist: what a lovely thing! Wraps and strands sallied back thusly. It was gay. The children were darling. Thump, thrump, thoom—they reached the avenue. (The trunk was taken to the harbor.)

THE NEPHEW

Well, yes, all right—woe. It is true: their lives had already gone by. But, moreover, there was the knurl in the collar of his shirt. A part poorly sewn. A bow tie. Pomade.

Well, yes—the sorrow to see them. It was the morning—this we know. It was not a perfect day. Oh, the shivering, in fact—and the worry. The wedding was made the way her mother's wedding had been made. It is foolish of us, after all: a knoll, the coaches—this notion, in other words, of something old.

Yes, of course—and the matter of the altar. The ghastly slit of sleeve touched her arm. The family stood in a row, henceforward. The flowers shuddered as such. He touched his mother's gown. (There was a tiny mark.)

THE NIECES

The Brussels lace was lost. Is it necessary to mention the wicks? (They were bitter.) The dale? (It was green.) The waltz? (What a happy thing!) Children threw rocks at the tails of a coat. Men were shooting ducks: oh, my goodness! The groom swooned.

But where were they standing? But what does it mean, the touching of the arm? They came down the aisle with mice at their feet. Is that the song? (It was dreadful, naturally, the way the steeple and the hill vanished behind the bend forever.)

Well, nevertheless—the trilly cobs, the veins: and, heavens, the thin ribs. But may we return to the girls?

To the groom's voice? (It was awful, the sound his name made.)

THE SISTERS

Here!—the horrible shapes in the creases of the blouse. The tragic jut of the plumes. The amusing history of the hobble skirt. (The sisters went away afterward, in other words.)

Bathing robes for hire—a sign—and caps, of course. It was warm there—and the water, the trees along the avenue, the little flapping, sometimes, in the shop awnings. (The bride and groom went to Lorouse.)

Chatter and a sigh, a cough, as it happens— chocolate, oh, dear, these dirty hands, these sleeves, something just a bit torn, after all, tucked in, folded, turned back, flattened. He was small and still a little cold. (The ladies came and played whist every afternoon.)

But yes, naturally—the threshold. It was fine inside. It was nice and warm, all right: the mouse and safe and sound. Is that the song? She had had a plum, anyway, and a truffle—one day when she was eight.

The slant of her neck!: and the pock was dark. The hoop had a strap and a shiny hook. What a grave event! The bride's was—her mother said—as narrow as a swallow's.

Well, the pall in the bother—the gnaw and mewl, so to speak, in the wool. The terrifying stoop, the color at the windows, an odor. Mercy, how it was stopped (and settled).

THE AUNTS

This, then, was the last one. The bed was curtained this way—with, perhaps, birds and a fawn. There was simply a drooping post, drapery facing. There was no blood. Shall we put it another way? Oh, that it was not you.

16

Such gloom!, for instance, and the frame, the town. But let us not be foolish. It is gone, this is all—and, nevertheless, the long hallway, the valance, the windowsill.

Does she recall the visit? The brocade? But certainly the curls? How he loved her! However, however—she left him. One went blind. One misplaced a bracelet. One sat for a portrait.

There was a sound at the stairs.

The sisters went away on holiday. They were old. The maids would steal from them.

The sisters kept cut flowers in a vase.

Blossoms, smell, spew.

It was, finally, nothing.

They took their meals in the room. They watched the ships at the window. They shut the trunk tight.

The sisters stayed there for a long time.

Rain, rain, rain. Soldiers walking by slowly in the street. The sound of the dumbwaiter down the corridor. Various glances and asides, pauses. A cleft in the tablecloth. A thumb pressed to the edge of the plate. (There was something rather troubling.) The shade clicked; the afternoon passed. Isn't it nice to think of the bibelots and the window swags, the bottles of milk in a tin box on the doorstep? Isn't it nice to wave to the neighbor, to walk the girls home? Rain, rain, rain. But the boughs and the groves. But does it matter what they would wear? Was the wool so gloomy, actually, clutched as it was? Only something concerning, say, a particular color. Simply the curve in the sleeve when she turned. Just a tender kind of muddling. A small breeze. The sound of the dumbwaiter down the corridor. (It was not for them a great regret, let us admit.) They ate supper; they played the radio. A wedding party walked by in the street. Yes: and it rained.

Mrs. Schwartz's dish showed a winter scene. Some hunters, a fellow in a Franz Josef hat, a gash in the blankets on a sleigh. A caller stood at a door in the next town. (There were terrible things out there, you see.)

The trunk had dates written on the spot where the slat was white. Chopped camphor, something wrung—wire through a hole in the shelf. There was a space betwixt, so to speak, the T and the Z. (Perhaps it seemed peculiar.)

A bracelet was dotted here and there. There were a few gems, apparently of a minor sort. Eyeglasses, acacia gum, letters. (A mention of places in Russia: Nevsky Prospekt, for instance, bent in the manner of "a buckling body.")

But the room, to return: there was scrollwork. One of the paintings showed a cheery tracery. Sylphs, sculpture, part of a lawn through a window. A linnet (shall we say) stood near the harrow in the lane. (The prefect was "a legendary failure.")

And as for the rest of the country: wouldn't it be fine to stay in a village on the island? Well, it was just that story or another one. They built forts; they rolled the cannon up the hill. The cavalry went to a dance. The captain wore a blue uniform with yellow epaulets; he held a riding crop. But the Dutch landed at the end of the year. (They brought the plague.)

The sun was sometimes so red and low in Spain. Isn't there, too, a myth about the water? Imagine her horror of the shoreline. The discussion of the waves. The lovely lapping sound. (The sisters drew a plain face in the dust of the dressing table.) Isn't it horrible to see the tile roofs, the screened porches, the pails of seashells? Well, all the women on the seashore. Yes: and the parasols on Sundays, street lamps, striped awnings, people stopping at each window. (The sisters fretted; they soaked their rings in a stockpot.) But there were pretty parts as well, weren't there? But weren't there flits of light, for instance, along the floor? The wallpaper had a pattern of shapes and circles, lines. Hurricane lanterns were arranged on the windowsill. (They caught a water

21

bug.) The maids would bring sliced fruit (an orange and a cantaloupe); they would run the bath. Sometimes the trees made a pleasant sound. Sometimes there was a moon in Spain.

It was a curiosity: peaches were bad that season, so mealy. It is cruel: there was a death, once, on her birthday. And this rustle in the blouse—the little curls, clotted bust. Her story about witches. Why, the bare wrist, the bit of bone. The thumb pressed to a cleft in the tablecloth (but across the faces of the fishes, gracious goodness, cleaving the eyes).

But simply a question of the place: it is better to think of it this way, isn't it? Soldiers would walk by slowly every morning. Clack, clack, clack, clack. Boats would wreck off the bluffs, years ago. Well, that was that. Notice the ancient burial caves. Statements about the nature of the engravings on the tombs, in any event. (And the tale of how the Inquisition began.)

But simply their history: the sisters were born in America. There were the beautiful portraits. The letters ("quean," or a word of this kind, and "love as ever"); the party (nobody, of course, had come); the lineage (one on this side, none on the other). Rosh Hashanah and girlish hats, purses. Coins loose about

the room. (Highness this or that—buttons.) But wouldn't it have been nice, riding horses? Quince, once—and foliage, pumpkins. The skating on the pond. (The girls fell down and all the people laughed.)

And as for other of the items: the photograph showed a fellow in knickerbockers. He stood near a bale of hay, a pheasant. There was a book concerning a Pole who had known three kings. He was rich when he was young; he was poor when he was old. A map: the church was here; the monastery was there. Seville was due south. (The mountains looked like wolves "in distress.")

The windowpane was cold. The windowsill was cold. The wall was cold. The lock was painted white. Dross and squeal, a tidy little print on the tablecloth. Dye came from Constantinople: isn't that it? Stems, vase water—tumblers. A terrible mistake, finally. Simply the wallet, the pretty paper money. The queer voices on the radio. (The shade clicked; the waves broke just so.)

Waves, waves, waves. She regretted that she had never looked properly at the sea. Yes, certain colorful effects—the delightful snap in the flags. Facts about the salt air. Various blunders were referred

to. (It was difficult, indeed.) Or just the unseemly posts. The dock. The aspects of the current: a good tide at this hour, a rough tide at that hour. But it could be so frightening, couldn't it? But a small breeze, haze. But to have had water behind the house, calf's-mouth in the garden, boots in a row. The correct place setting. A masquerade ball. (The sisters watched the ships at the window.) The ferry was a figure of great beauty, naturally, in the fog. There was a commotion in the square. The grass— the cannon. (The girls' dresses got caught in the fishnets, in crab traps.) Well, bait on the decks of the boats. The meandering. March and another month. Dates. The waves, of course, at night.

The sisters slept on their backs.

Shh.

There was the sound of the dumbwaiter down the corridor.

The sisters kept a comb, a jar of sweets on the dressing table. They kept the drawer shut.

The trunk was taken out in the morning.

The *Godless* florin, which was first issued in 1807, and which is not especially rare, exhibits, on the obverse, a rather unflattering bust of Phillip the Pennyless—who, we now know, had been murdered near Bern. The lane was fine? Blood carts passed the tulips in the dark. The bottles resembled bones? A blanket covered the casket. The reverse exhibits a circle of shields, at the base of which, next to the figure of a spade, appear the engraver's initials. There are piercings, a cut edge. A reeded edge, I should say. The sickle-shaped incuse was once thought an emblem of the prince's regret.

The steward's tunic was discovered in 1825, at the foot of a pillory. Or, according to older accounts, at the lip of a broad ditch, among certain other remains. Ruins, that is. A Dutch grommet. A captain's chain. A siege piece. He had lain at the gate? The cold, it was said, had crept into the thorn-box. The hearts were excised on Collop Wednesday and Buzzard Sunday. Does the color green not please you? The cleaver had a rosewood handle. Beneath the copper pot was an altar cloth. Dun-colored, I believe. It was bad luck for blood to touch the shroud.

The lord provost's mourning flag was stolen in 1844. The flag was red, which strikes me as rather odd. Little is made of the tower-pike, however, except in respect of the inscription, the seal inscription, whose point is, indeed, worrisome—if you will forgive the graceless phrasing. Little is made of the weather vane, of the gables, of the steeples. Oh, all my dismal lists. His eyes, it seems, had been eaten by ants. Bowls of witches' hair had been placed in trenches. The beadle fell to his knees in grief? Edward was afraid. Knobs of burnt wood were discovered, with the hooves of the bellman's cow, in a rabbit warren. The shape of the flag, incidentally, was often likened to the shape of a poke bonnet, which pleases me— even if the fact of the rowboat has never quite been explained. The duck blind, still and all, the choke-cherry and the maw, a bit of a squawk in the lake— the matter is always left at that. His hens, it seems, had been caught at the door and mauled. There were goats, lest we forget. A crowd in the courtyard.

How old is your father? Do you miss your brother? The hangman's name escapes me at the moment. The document was in Latin. Among the possessions were a surplice and a crozier, antique greaves, a seam of fodder—and his mother's widow's weeds. The hood and a halved penny were bequeathed to his wife.

The 1858 *Arms,* issued in commemoration of Long Friday, exhibits, against a gray field, a portrait of Miss Mary Linwood—who, on the Brenner Pass, had swallowed a pretty silver lock. There were clouds in the background? Birds? She was the niece of a priest. A dog howled in the palace? Let us make an accommodation for the hour. There was a blizzard on Pauper Saturday? Certain matrons died in a Moorish town. Beneath the name appears the figure of a bonfire. Beneath the mantle appears the figure of a belfry. Beneath the date appears the figure of Janus in agony. There are small faults, a full black strike.

The *King* triptych, auctioned in 1882, exhibits, in its center panel, a coach-and-six, a post chaise-and-four, constables two-and-two. The map is inexact. The balcony is often thought too sentimental a figure. And that is that? So it is. Save for the scarlet runners. Save for the fountain. The archbishop of Pritchard— whose geese are apparent in the foreground—was poisoned by a parishioner. The river breaks? There was a slaughter in the midst of a thundershower. A massacre, rather. One sunny day. They burned the flax and tow. Tongues were nailed to the deacon's door. Our observer prefers to avert his eyes? The final sermon referred to the margrave's sorrow—and to the margravine's departure in the fall.

Mother takes child on a visit. Towns, you understand. Cottages. The evening meal.

February, yes? March?

Cornish hens or a stew. Bliss potatoes. Cabbage. Artichoke hearts.

There are parcels, as well?

Gifts. Gifts. Yes—it seems so. Spectacles, perhaps. Perhaps an article of clothing.

There is a muffler at the throat, is there not?

Merely the drizzle and the rail. Merely these puddles in the road.

Oh—March, indeed.

A lamb chop or a roast. Olives—green olives. Beets, actually. Swedish turnips. A Spanish onion for the trash.

She points heavenward?

Granted—there is red ribbon. Cuff links or a pocket watch, after all. The pears are overripe. The bread is burnt.

There is a fresh tablecloth, is there not?

Merely a view of the lake. Merely a view of the pikes and the dock. Towns, you understand.

Claws? Casters?

Mother trims neatly the fat from the meat.

Daybook. Certain of the dates are incorrect. Surely they are. The month—the months. The maiden name is misspelled. These addresses are old. Squares and dashes, a column. Yes—a routine, I see. Oh, dear. The train fare and the cost of the meal. A raffle. The post office and the bank.

The inheritance was of little consequence.

There is a puncture—a hole, if you would prefer. "Decedent died without issue"? One of the daughters, I gather, had never married. The son had recovered. No—that is a bit misleading. The casket was cheap. They rarely visited the father's family. Whereas the dahlias? The plot faces east.

Deed. Beating the bounds, I see. Beating away the moths. It was the view, after all. Or a rift of sorts. Such a quaint way to put it. "Beginning at this point in the northwest corner." Well. The roofs were red, in any event. One and the next. We must do without a dark courtyard, must we not? All the roads, pell-mell. One chain, one link to a stake. And a staircase—to which they would repair.

30

Daybook. Certain initials, if you will abide this. An aunt's address. The brother at a peculiar hour. Reft— is this the word? Or smote? Lunch was late. Yes— the butcher's paper. A teapot, I expect. Now quite empty, indeed. Plaid skirts and black stockings. Or brick houses and a privet.

The itinerary was thought a separate matter.

The following week, the following month, the New Year. Simply a description of his loneliness, you could say. "Tilbury Fright"? Tilbury Fort on Tilbury Plain. On the date of a cessation. Of a dissolution, rather. Its anniversary, in any event. Oh, an outing, a walk, a tour. There was better weather in the end.

The gloves were given first. They were soft, yes, and small—but there was a tear. The worsted—one of his—and the houndstooth—a wound, here—were lost. Or set aside, if you will oblige me.

What of the buttoning, the buckling, the seam?

There was a feather duster for the far shelf. And pins—plain pins. The cribbage table had a false drawer. The box was diamond-shaped—with a cleft hinge. There was a note in a violet envelope.

This rescues the figure, does it not?

The handbag was blue—a plump, picturesque object, the clasp of which was scuffed. The muffler was red. The blouse—a birthday, perhaps—had an odd weave—or, anyway, a loop came up. There were clips in the sheet, hooks in the eyes, wax.

There was a padlock for the chest.

Inventory. In a small hand. Yes—objects of the father's. Objects of the uncle's—or of the wife's, if you would prefer. Shall we consider the cellar? Omitting the unmentionables, then. Omitting the middle terms. Scissors and a basin, the faces of the plates. A bottle of witch hazel. The prettiness of the clothespress.

But to emend this a bit.

The brother lay here. Have I mentioned the handsome little shadows? There were squirrels in the walls. The aunts sat in these chairs. Coleworts, Silesia lettuce, wine. The rug was gray. The table-cloth was ragged, I am afraid. The teaspoons had been disarranged, given away.

Announcement. "The bride cries because she must go." One of the daughters wept at the door. For hours? Perhaps not. Counting the pillars, if nothing else. Counting finials, newels. The sheet seemed a trifling thing. Yet the color, once again—or simply the crease. An attendant, a cousin of the groom, tripped on the steps. The maid of honor, a cousin of the bride, dropped a bouquet in the aisle.

Inventory. Ruined bloomers, dyed red. Cuff links. A Brussels-lace mantilla. Doubtless the new shoes and the new dress. There was, I suspect, a spot of turn and-ruffle, a question concerning the stitch. Not to mention a hopeful glimpse of the lawn—or of, rather, the trees, the length of the path.

That is a touch melodramatic, however.

She was staring at her hands. The coat was pulled closed. The walk was dark? The aunts stood in the road. Silver buttons and a pendant, the dismal dots on the wall. A bottle of squill. The old linens. Certain of the names, I should add, are circled. The A is slender. The S breaks.

Let me apologize for the rain. Indeed—such cold, such great wind. The rotted portion of the pike, now—and the slip, the very shape of it. There was a hatbox in the lake.

Have I stated this adequately?

We must do without a gannet, without a thrush.

Let me attend, instead, to the road. The cottages, a few of them, had burned down. As had the bell tower. The gates had been razed. There were branches and tassels on the knoll.

Oh, the falling, all the falling—this you must surely recall.

33

The dock was black. As was the pike. The rowboats were brown—which is for the best, or, in any event, not unpleasant—yes, quite fitting, quite apt, really, at such an hour.

The mist—the fog—puts the matter to rest.

Daybook. A grievous evening. This will do. A number and a phrase—certain items in this vein. There were souvenirs, I trust. Or mistakes of a sort. Think of it: he had not—he had never—known. "My dear Mesdames"? "My dear Mssrs."? Mercy. I have forgotten other of the visits. I have neglected them, rather.

A woollen blanket was missing.

A silk handkerchief was soiled.

The tailor's in the morning? In the afternoon, actually. Or the seamstress, the seamstress. And then the butcher shop. All the changes, in gray. Or once and for all. "The lines have fallen upon me." Their meal, her departure, his return. The new linens had been stolen. The porch awning was white.

Deed. The house was brick—and had tall windows, black shutters, and, next to the front door, a lamp, the glass of which was cracked. The knocker was brass. The hallway—shall we pause here a moment? Parcel gilt, perhaps. Knuckle hinges and a tulip rail. The staircase was notable for its sadness. But there now——no, no. I will begin again. A view of the snow, we may suppose. Rabbits ran across the grass, east to west. The walk was dark. The knocker was brass. There was a second lock, a dead bolt.

Daybook. Saving the gloves. Saving the hats. Hanging the dresses. Visiting all the windows, I see. A bed of leaves——this does seem a pleasant thing to suggest. The dahlias died. Whereas the privet? The cellar door was of little distraction. The wives——if memory serves——did not wave.

Have I mentioned the bracelet? The pocket watch? The ring was sold.

Certain of the names are crossed off. "Nothing sticks to the child's ribs." They sat together. Buzzard——this must be the word. Leaving the party for the pantry. And the other address, in due course. "Regards." "Our love." Just the odds and ends. She saw to the sugar, to the spill, to the bones.

She held the pin out in the light, I like to think—— the door of the sitting room, this tiny room, shut—— a garment slipping from her knees.

The chair, you understand, the chairs——simply the older ones.

There was an embroidered footstool. The cribbage table had oak spindles, an oak throat. The tea cart was thought delightful—or sufficient, in any event. There was a wooden paperweight for the far shelf.

I wish to be thorough.

A quilt—the child's, perhaps—was folded like so. There was a joke concerning the color, the flesh of a plum. The prunella—wrung—and the cowl—with burl—had bled into the bend.

Inventory. A note and a deed, statements. Doubtless all the drawers. A good week, I believe. Oh, or a very bad one. Tea biscuits for dessert, at least. A bit of mildew here and about. Facts concerning a rosette and a napkin, the candlestick at her feet. It appears the ginger root had resembled a man. Or the wood had. The lamb collops, for their part, had been discarded neck and crop.

The aunts crossed the road.

I have neglected the rest of the family, I am embarrassed to say.

The nephew died first. All the suitors were poor. The sisters were not intimate. Well. There was something on a Sunday, as it happens. She had asked for an ash casket. Evidently the husband arrived, this time, in the afternoon, late in the afternoon. Early in the evening, really.

Itinerary. The chest was locked in the morning. They stayed the day. "State Street." Hampshire Avenue. Quite a surprise. An address at the black house, as the expression has it. Consider, instead, the clouds, the spires, the signatures. "Milk Street Market." The scenery, such as it is. Please stand here near the grass. Dripping awnings, wail, down. You can see the petunias are going well now. The bedroom did not face the lake. New Street is pretty in the snow? The other plans had been cancelled.

Inventory. The cellar shelves. A bottle of rose water. Linens on the lawn. Her mother's, I gather, was another month. Granted—the rocks were not a pleasant prospect. Nor was the oak. Just a choice of sorts. Yes—this side or that. Something small was offered? The gesture struck them as antique.

She crossed her legs.

These shoes and a handbag. A lemon tart, on second thought. A baked apple. This was all. Pitted peaches, hulled strawberries, coffee. How foolish I am. The bracelet, at least, was saved. The basin was clean. The drapery hung thus. Doubtless the house was quiet at that hour.

Father departs. True enough. Here is the train depot.

In the rain?

Crabgrass and thorns, a thoroughfare. A field, now—a portion of a field.

There is a hat, is there not?

Why, fine breezes. A row of holes, you understand. Danes' blood. Lady's smock. Lady Sally's demise.

He regards the birds?

Merely the flags—gray, white—and the lamps. These clouds. Merely the trestle—at length.

The moon at an odd moment.

Thistle and simmer. Fireweed, actually. Bark—a modest patch of it.

Have we, then, the wrong season?

Oh—the shape of the brim, the shape of the crown. The color of the band.

The flags fail?

Feverfew for yarrow, you understand. Or for fennel. A row of posts.

The train reaches the trees.

BLINDSTITCH

I discard the blue woollen gloves, the white bowls, the beeswax candles.

On the doorstep is a tin box for the bottles of milk. In the dining room is a wooden table in an oval shape.

Well, well.

The breakfront creaks.

I wash the mirrors with vinegar and hot water. I tidy the shelves.

On the table are plates: olive pits, stemmed figs, June peas. Leaves of cabbage and the spine of a perch. Keen knives.

There is a lurch in the curtain.

The window is a bow window? There is a fine view of the latticework. A shadow halves the path? The porch door? There is, as well, a fine view of the trees. But what of the picket? There is something in the very turn of it, if you wish. The lawn—the street. Now a polite little gate? The latticework is brown.

I fold the tablecloth in a comely way.

On the tea cart is a napkin. On the sideboard are the larger of the saucers, the smaller of the teapots, a saltcellar.

A portrait rattles on a brad.

I arrange the armchairs thus, at the far wall.

The hat stand and the fire screen are old. The newel is dull.

In the hallway are chests, a candlestand.

On the bedroom floor are moths.

The porch door is locked. Let us do without the sunlit portion of the lawn, without the wrought-iron bench. The trees are, indeed, locust trees? Let us regard the birds, first—or, say, the husband's hat. It has a narrow brim, a bent, punctured crown. It was a gift, you know. As was, incidentally, this ornament on the wall. The ottoman is red. Whereas the wife's housedress? Her nightdress? These empty flowerpots, actually. A patch of something: this is better still. And now the cut ribs in the green, let us imagine—a trembling in the hedge, a gruesome blue. But that overstates it a bit. Mums for the fall, then. Common thorns. Do recall, if you will, the flush in the wife's face. The apron is frayed? The candlesticks have cracked, alas. Yes—let us note the table, the kind of table, the style of it. Anyway, the trestle's peculiar fluting. Edward's eye: is this the term? Let us settle for it. The ottoman was a concession of sorts, you know. The husband's hat was a gift. As was this object of the child's? Such a meager example, one is afraid. The trees, incidentally, are birch trees. Do forgive the wind, the breach in the leaves, the rail along the path. Moreover, the bolt is rusted—and the latch is black.

The moths are gray.

September, even early September, excludes the coffin flies and certain of the spiders. The bloodroot is of less concern.

A riflebird is mistaken for a thrush— or for a grackle, rather. It is the mask, plainly—or perhaps the shriek.

A plummet is mistaken for a plunge.

The spikes explain the mantle, the curious form of it, and the pattern in the plumage—which, in turn, explain the fuss.

The ten-lined Jane, its shell, explains the flesh flies and the creeper—if not the width of the veins in the wings.

The yellow bones click.

The house faces south. Is this correct? There is an arch. There are fissures in the path. The porch gets the sun at this hour, you know. Whereas the wrought-iron bench? The armchairs, incidentally, are Queen Anne armchairs. There are knots in the legs of the ottoman. The husband stands before the vanity drawer? Let us regard the doorframe, first—just the shadows there. Dust squalls the length of the doleful little ledge. Quite a claim. This hinge is without a claw? Evidently the tea service is without a creamer. The saltcellar is porcelain. It has a bell-shaped silver handle. The trestle is tulipwood: this is discreet enough an appraisal, you will agree. Yes—the top before the bars. Or the stout bit of scrollwork, the unflattering burl. The ornament is quaint, is it not? Whereas the candlesnuffer? The wife's housedress is blue. The blouse has a scalloped collar. It seems we have neglected the needlepoint, however—and the child's bed. The shelves are pine. These are daisies on the wallpaper? In addition, let us imagine. Doubtless certain of the trees are diseased. A shadow halves the path. There are stones in a row, a gate. One of the shutters is shut.

The street curves? Wall begins at the corner and ends at Broad. New crosses Prospect and Union. There is a diverting climb the next mile? Park begins here, modestly, and crosses Center and High. The latter narrows? Market is homely in the heat.

I see to the sheets.

I see to the quilt.

On the bureau are keys—and a lamp with a glass shade.

The wardrobe stands at the near wall.

The dowel sags.

In the hallway are chests, a pair of brass doorstops, a rug.

The newel is dull.

On the tea cart are tumblers, the newer of the tumblers.

The table hobbles.

I soak the rags in the sink.

A GERMAN
PICTURESQUE

CONFESSION

The goblet, to begin with. There are a few trees, a few hills, rows of trefoil. The flag is white, or, put differently, as white as the devil "in his feathers"—discovered, it is understood, in error, or by surprise, next to the creel and the bowl of gruel and the cuckoopint.

The coaches are blue, if it pleases you.

The bell is thought poorly drawn—except for the neck, a portion of the neck—except for a portion of the haunch, which is thought genteel, and beneath which appears, in roman letters, the motto. The confession, for its part, addresses the inconveniences of bloodletting and the dreariness of embroidering wool—even if there is little mention, here, of the uniform, of the heart, of the pine box.

GATE

A mourner mentions the surname—and, less to the point, the linnet, the handsomeness of its demise. The horses step on dormice. Notice how certain of the dogs seem to resemble common bronze urns. Disregard, though, the ward's digression upon blindness—and the abundance of fur in the grass.

WILL

Next to the trees appear the insignia and the dates—the years, in any event—and a description of another affliction, which is fitting, if you will pardon the phrase, given how it recalls the skinned rabbit and the draggled eggs on the scaffold. The blanket's crease, of course, was thought insufficient—the curve of it perplexing in a way, the bodies tiny, so terribly so.

But having said this.

The arms are per pale—the scroll, first, and then the skull, just the horns and the spine and, in shadow, the dagger. The will addresses the other

46

will—merely the "commencement" of the death; merely a mattock and Saint Gregory's purgatory— if not the pearl onions in drills.

LANE

You might object that this omits the widow. To be specific: the posts are black. There are boll weevils and a stone wall, creeping eaves. If the mutes are hidden behind the privet—well, then naturally the matter is much simpler.

ERRATA

Consider that the older goblet had been immured, with certain persons, and with a handbell and a poniard, at a nunnery in Worms. All the martlets—dexter tierce, gules—"perch like amulets," or fatten, in any event, and darken, whereas the eagles at the edges—sinister tierce, displayed, sable—"die." Yes, yes—and the likeness rises, in a manner of speaking, the collar covered with a strip of cloth, a neat seam—which covers, as well, a portion of the month, the conjecture and the errata, and, moreover, the emblem—for which there is little affection.

DRAWBRIDGE

There is great affection for the route, the same route, this bit of it, and—given the season— for the color of the leaves and of the water, which breaks "unquietly," repairing "to the gash"—recalling, it is thought, the figure of carts departing a castle, "as white as white periwigs," just this, the rest of a procession or the last of one.

You will excuse the extravagance.

There are drapes on the doors, paths before the gardens. There are meadows, slowly but slowly. Notice how—in this light—the chains conceal the anvil. Notice how the cattle in the background might be mistaken for clouds.

The heart had been embalmed and, "enshrined in an unlovely goblet," brought to the elder daughter. Consider the flesh, the notion of the flesh, the notion of the cinders—swept on, as it were, this way—the brothers missing, the widow wearing violet, a cawl of silver fallen at the shoulder. Perhaps the emblem is sorrowful, then—or, in lieu of this, sullen. After all, there were ruins of a kind: a salver, a "singular" pickax, the uniform. A history addresses the epaulets, which had been soaked in lye and burned, and laments the damage to the cottage— or to the cellar, rather—where the children were starved.

TOWNS

The map is adequate for the occasion, indicating, at center, the roads and the towns, a drawbridge, the river—and, more discreetly, at bottom, the location of certain graves. The color of the lane recalls the color of the noose—at least in respect of the servant, who, all the while, had held a velvet cushion—which was heart-shaped, no less, and crimson.

ADDENDA

The family had not been massacred. This was, in fact, something of an exaggeration. The attendants had wept "upon the bodkins," however—and skeletons had been trundled from house to house. There were choke pears and Dutch tongues, thatches. The feathers had paid for the goose, in a manner of speaking—or, more likely, for the rings, which, with a silver brooch, had been lost in the mud. There was a list of wishes. There was an arrangement by days. Still, the archbishop's miter does little to explain the betrayal—or, for that matter, the finches atop the pine box.

GATE

A mourner mentions the widow's shadow. Horses fall. Notice the brood sow at the tower house, the fissures at the choristers' feet. Notice that the mutes' throats are exposed. Disregard, though, the ward's coy way of counting the wounds.

EULOGY

The goblet had been purchased on the anniversary of a poisoning, then sold—or stolen—in Sasbach, and recovered—or exhumed—in Bonn. The stem, a portion of it, is red. There is brown cross-hatching at the base.

There are beehives behind the gravestones.

The flag is thought inelegant—given the tear in the canton, at the clutch—and given the surname's turn, certain marks beneath the letters. The motto, moreover, neglects the death itself: there are scarlet runners and calves' blood, a curious description of the hills. Ostrich plumes, cropped ostrich plumes, are addressed in the eulogy—the beginning of which, concerning the beckoning, is read at the end.

II

O X

So the train ride down. Slyo, Blokes, Varn, Neel, Sir, Hels, Helding, Harm, Bonelawn, and Starvation Peak. Bolts, flaps, lorns, tanks, steens, bears, knife ties—the slag on the roadbed, a boy in a berth. Passing: bullrings, the gate route, the buttress, the light. On the platform are pumps, a fellow selling food, a priest next to a post. In history: men would shoot game from the moving windows. Grasshoppers would cover the track. The family had top East and family ancestors. The root in the caboose was the crummy. A cripple was bad. In the berth: the curtain blows, all right. You can see behind me how the house goes. He holds my hand. The berts, spinks, spears—and you bark your shin! Troutville has mountains named for the suffering of the settlers. Nosaje has mines and the largest graveyard in America. All the kinsmen were killed by red Indians. Or all the children had the croup. (Or a train got stuck in the mud under the water.) We eat: river-snap stringbeans. Geet-rind sweet asparagus. Mint-jar olive snipe. Stuffed duck. A chop. The other man there is a sailor. We pass: the lady in the lambhouse, for example. The girl in the curled-up thicket. Docks next to the wrecks. Birds: that is a big-boned rover, normally found in warmer climes. This is an open-collared marbink. A few lose their wings at one hundred feet—and sink. Inside the train there are blue suitcases, a blue valise, a blue hatbox. There are letters and numbers on a wooden trunk. In the berth there are other blue things. They cross at the bottom—thin ones and the one that is thick. Everything is dark. A train is a safe place. On the train a fellow sells fruit and bread. The eyeskin is pinched and squinted on the rip. A lady waits at a door. (Father helps her through.) This is the view from the caboose. The highball means everything is all right. In history: the caboose comes loose. The first locomotive was built in a hollow in England. The man used this pig iron. People said the first locomotive looked like his mother's body! This part was the feather and this part was the hat. This is the way into the city. At the outskirts her skirts come up—the buckles, the post. He runs to the rail. He swings his arms largely. He waves his hat. We lean over. There is a way to fall down and die in a doorway, you see. Armstrong,

Happy Valley, Stink River. Passing: track. The animals run on the river sand, one by one. Skulls on the sidings are the real thing. This is the street with the house that looks like ours. This is a knot of the sort in the West, on the dog or on the ox slipping on the ice, all that weight tied on. The head was wet. The hooves came through the roof. There were sticks on the railroad—and a pick. There was a great and giant train: boxcar, flatcar, hopper, gondola, stock, caboose. Gravel, grain, rock, cinder, bulb, frog. The boy, the boy, the boy. I wish I knew the names of the places. The hole in the berth, the curtain. We come through the thicket fast. There he is! He puts up the box. He pulls down along the silver rim. He holds his hand. He breathes.

And so the train glides into Chicago, on the sidings and the break. Oh, the train ride into Chicago—the hose, the highball, the backs of houses, the lot. We went down. We held the rail. We held the porter's hand. There was a cart at the station—next to a yellow train in the snow. There were boys running on the track—falling off for who falls off first. They sold food at a stand, and hats. Father walked. Mother said the niggers. The boy dropped all the bags. Was it the oak stick that got stuck and kept? Was it the cut in the cheek and the green? Did he see the one broken-open contour on the handle of the door? No. (But Father did.) The boy dropped on himself half the bags. Through the broken part in the fence the boy in the yards lost a ball through the broken part in his arms and the ball rolled through the broken part in the fence to you. We went: across the platform, across the track, off the roadbed, along the bank, along the rail, along the aisle, up the stair.

Into the berth. We roll so slowly out of Chicago, over the sidings, over the snow, over the cracked black break. In history: a train could be brought in dead. In history: they would hang men from the caboose. The porter would pull the curtain. The porter is coming closer. He keeps the stick straight and clean. He touches a spot on the wall. Everything is quiet. You can see the vase, the bottle, the bucket. You can see how he stands and the way the town falls down. Here is the rip. The curtain is balled at the bottom and turned back, bunched through a ring. There is a sound above a boy in Virginia. We eat: peas, carrots, cream. Green-sleeve heart beans. Three potatoes: boiled white, baked white, and the red marshmallowed sweet. He eats succotash. She eats black marrow. One cucumber sliced long. The cut-cut of meat. She says we are eating off spoons that a cardinal once used. The other man's father died the day he came home from the war. We pass a train passing. (A truck-train passes us.) The rocks' color comes from the blood of an animal. On the fifteenth day of July 1861 said Confederates stop a train. The colonel shoots you blindfolded, around his back. Certain settlers used the bones of their children to build houses. The sleepy conductor waves to the sleepy people. In the berth: you watch the sot on the window drop—water or mud or breath. You make the zag under the tower's churt, the bar of the gang brush, the bell circle and the birch, her cheek, her teeth, her tongue. Mother loves me! The porter holds the bolt. He breaks the bed down. He sets the sheets. We pass: Elephant Battle, Fort Bliss, Big Hatchet Park. The hank of a boat in the wood. A cornfield meet. The nearest, largest barn. A house with the top chopped off. He stands next to me. He turns back the blanket. He pulls the sheet that you can see the white. He pulls in the packet sleeve. There is the little bend, and then—I do not know! The family sleeps through the night. We eat: chunks of hot bread. A ham with a hole inside. An orange on a plate. There is a brown cut left—and this melon, wet leaves, some berries, and fat. The butter is bad. A glass falls to the floor. In history: there was a dead man for breakfast every morning. In a wooden trunk on the train there are coats, dresses, scarves, and a blue suit and shoes. She says these men will eat me from the feet up! He says all the names. We reach the graveyard in Farmingdale. You sit down and begin to shiver. Everything is all right. These are the holes. They say the rustle you see is a mouse. He shows me the birds. A blackpoll is a warbler. The feathers on the head are black. This is a brokenhearted pinbird. It is hard—that is a tree or a cow or a man out there. On the train they say Mother is lovely. She kisses me hard on the cheek. Mother had the croup when she was a girl. (Mother had a girl.) In history: the boy was born. He goes East and through. Oh, the train ride home! In the station the curtain tugs and you can see the curve in the nub. The man is standing next to the woman. The boy kneels. The train brakes.

A GRAMMAR

I would touch a spot on the sheet.
I would touch the windows and the grass, the rip
beneath the trees, by the boat—which, indeed, was
sinking. The mountain in the bracken was the face,
and pleasant, pertaining also to the pitter-patter in
the walls, to farce, that is to say—at least inasmuch
as the headboard was oxblood, but not old, and the
door, of a sudden, was open.

The water pitcher, given an accident of the shadows, resembled a woman—the fact of which recalls,
oddly, the little book in the bookcase, a grammar,
or, at any rate, the coats in the closet—and the
woman who, quietly, parenthetically, oh, yes, later
on, at the end, said your name.

I would touch the spot that felt like skin, the
shards of thread on the part that made his arms,
the horsehair stuck through the mountain and the
fields—which were quite black in aspect, it now
seems. I would touch where it was warm, it is true,
the crease loose, my sleeve a little clumsy, a little

bunched and to the side—worn, in short, poorly, the tumbler like so, the moment undone.

The birch trees are indistinct. (It is dusk, after all.) There is a lawn. (Wrought-iron gate, lamps.) A fellow calls to a dog. (The mailbox stands next to the fence.) An automobile passes. (You will note, just the same, the walk, the dark pots, the benches.) Mrs. Schwartz tends to the flowers. (Now she turns, and we cannot see her anymore.)

One considers the pattern, frets over it, sets it out in the light.

The interval, you will agree, is droll.

The soldier, whose boots are shining, the wool of whose uniform is blue, rides beyond the farmhouse.

The man and the woman are off to town, possibly—to buy, one likes to think, eggs and such, buttermilk, sugar, a loaf of bread.

There is something bedeviling about the error.

The bonnet, for instance, is apparent and then hidden.

Oh, there is a sort of trill, one confesses—and, why, a dwindling.

———

A curtain rustles somewhat. (It is the cat, of cour
Music plays. (*Falstaff,* or something to this effec
Doors are opened and closed. (Earrings sit upon a
end table.) Objects are clutched, arranged, observed
(The moon—to digress—is gone.)

The chifforobe, upon which was emblazoned, in red,
a lake scene (birds—apple trees), and upon a shelf of
which would sit his cuff links, stood next to the
nightstand—and at some remove from the window.
The bed was a curious example of the Colonial four-
poster style, one is told, on account of the claw-and-
ball feet—and the squeal, in a manner of speaking,
in the frame.

    The quilt was kept at the foot, at the posts, or, to
be precise, where I had made the rows of trees and
pickets his legs on the sheet. The chair, which was
maplewood, and scuffed rather variously, had embroidered arms and a discolored rib, and sat next to
the bed, yes, and against the wall—through which,
you understand, would sometimes come a bit of this
or that.

There are ducks and boats. (Gifts, after all.) The
bookcase is black. (The windowsill is brown.) The

chifforobe stands across from the closet. (Collars, buttons, shoes.) Pictures hang above the desk. (Elephants and knots, plainly.) The door is open. (You will note, moreover, the flannel, the hole.)

He pulls the sheet to my neck.

OCTAVE

The leaves deceive us. Likewise the knives. Think, please, of the cribbage table, the legs of which hobble a trifle, and rattle—and a drawer of which is false. The pine is white? The family was standing in the parlor. The highboy has been dismantled, the wire turned out. The rug curls back at the corners. Pins sit in a long dish. I confess I am fond of the faience—and of, all the more, the flowers, these wax flowers, encased, as they are, in glass. Have you misgivings about the light? I am happy for a sound in the hallway. There is camphor in the chests, on the shelves. Pins—hatpins—sit in a long dish. The fire screen bleeds. I wish to apologize for the cabinet clock—which, as you are aware, has stopped. The knives sit side by side. Oh, well, yes— the other silver had been his, it is safe to say. Mrs. Schwartz fell at the door. Will you agree that the likeness is fine? The highboy has been dismantled, the wire turned out. Think, now, of the chairs, their carvings—and of the crimp at the top of the drape. The pine is white. There is camphor in the chests, on the shelves. The rug curls back at the corners. The leaves keen.

I depart the room rather charmlessly.

He stands by a wall. The wall is a brick wall. There is a crack. There are slats and slants left from the letters of boys' names. His sixteenth great-grandfather was executed by the elector of Saxony in the sixteenth century. His sixteenth great-grandfather became famous for his way of weeping. The family is named for the place. They went away by boat. They arrived safely. He claps shut the cuff of a sleeve. The groom wore a frock coat and a top hat. He tripped on the way to the wedding. He drowned in the Nevsky River. They put their mouths on the lung. They breathed into it. The sons would eat the bladder. A king was coming from Bleeds in Augsburg. It was lazy in Hazia. Or hazy in Lazia? They stayed. He once practiced a waltz with his father in a barn. He holds his heart in the heat. They put rocks atop a headstone. The plot is at Mount Ararat. This name comes from the word for quiet-and-early death. This is the great-nephew of the smallest man killed at the Battle of Visby. He did not trip over any of the graves. He turns. He has his back to us now. His father fought in a war. They put the guns to the soldiers' noses. There were calves' skulls in the windows. There was a dead cow in the road.

They called the names.

He falls.

You see the floor, the doorknob, a box you had when you were a boy. Here are the coins, the basket beneath the mirror. Here is the tiny wooden doggie on a stick. The table, the plate, and here it is, the hair at first and something small—oh, my. The bed things are folded—elephants, little by little, and the flannel, the stitch. There are ruined bed things, too—curled and cut. Here is the tiny wooden doggie in the middle, standing back or landing—crashing!—and its rope tail, your mother and father sitting in a room. The table, the plate, the hair at first, and here are the coins in the basket, this hat, his hand—clat and struck. Now you are saying I am old!—a train ride home, a day in the rain, horses across the wall in the huff of a field. Here are the blackberries we had for breakfast. Here is the burr of a bird. You see the floor, the wall, the basket beneath the mirror. His hand is bent this way. His hand comes open—and a twitch of her hair touches your face.

There were these things there.
A small scroll nailed into the doorpost. A cut in the wood of the door. A coat hanging next to a cart. A hat atop a box. She kept a basket of fruit in this room. He kept candles in the window for the holiday. There was a chair next to the wall. The chair had a curl. The chair had faces of angels on its back. It had lines carved into its arms. The table had a tusk. The box was kept on the floor. I want to remember the rest! Jesus Christ was turned here. I thought the thorns were worms. I thought the holes in the skin were bugs. The Cross was splintered and the post was split. The cloak was torn. There was a curve. Bumps of mud covered the bone. Men carried Him. Smoke came up. You could see bristle and a mark on the neck. The cloak looked wet. A dog was turned this way: it had a paw in the air. Mary was kneeling. It was the round part of the spoon on the flat, I suppose. There was a clacking, down. It was steam and jam, but a line, too: it had hair and hers. There were

veins from the knees. There was a hat atop a box. A chair was next to a cart. The painting hung on the wall. His coat hung here. There was hair from a horse sticking out through it.

There was a tree next to the house. The tree had cracked root and veng at the bottom of its trunk. There was a hole in the ground. There were sticks, stalks, balled vine, witchgrass, peat. Clumps of dirt and clay covered fat and thorny branches. The way a dead tree smells! The tree was the head; the house made the shape of God's body; God was holding His arms out around our house. Well—is this true? The hearse is the rock at the top of the staff, or it is His fist—He held a rock in the desert. There was wind. The men held a board of beef. They were running, or holding on to His feet, or falling down in their gowns. The length of the lights from the church is meant to show a part of God's body. The people weep in the street. We would walk back with an-other family. There was a baby in a carriage. The tree was next to the house. You would see the patch kept from the garden—and the path with the rag and the dath! The rocks were buried but the tops, scraped, up—next to the throat of the boy, up, yes, his sawed teeth, his buried legs, the poor boy's rope hands holding the name on wood of a family, up, these steps and up: Mother was at the window.

There was a story for the family: the son drowned on the way to the wedding. Men took the casket off the cart. Other men lifted the stirrup. They took the hood and the velvet—he was uncovered. The body was dirty. The street was wet. There were lamps on posts. There were the doors of a ballroom. The mother, the father, the daughter—they all walked. But they were run under horses—but the family died on the way to the graveyard! Moses took with them the bones of Joseph. I am not certain of the rest. Another ancestor of ours was executed. They took his clothing. He fell down before the men. He prayed to God. They threw rocks from the top of the fortress. His head sat upon a slab. His family ran from the house. They escaped by boat. They made the voyage safely. He would take me to the lake. There were trees from the house to the water. There were chips of bark. The dirt had pits. Bunches of rope were set on the grass. There were bugs inside a beaver. Bricks were wrecked and stacked atop the bricks. Here was the thumb when he put them through—you could see at the hem of the dress a crease from the breeze of you walking past. Father waved to me! The stem was in the palm, the bit slapping a gash and a lump on the back. Gnats came up—but there were no crocuses, no rat runts underneath, never skunks dead in dirt up to their necks. The porch ran along and broke at the end in latticework, drizzle, roof, birdhouse, and the sniff and white of cloth. This was another room there. Wood of the slat turned—and the corner from the window was marked. There was something here— small and worn, next to the bobbins, the scarves, the choker, the basket, and the wooden hook. There was a circle on the frame. This is another way to make the shape of Jesus Christ, I think. The priest keeps his arms in the air for certain prayers; God's breath pulls and stands at the candles; God leaves all the places He has been. There is a gesturing of the hands, they say, that is a way to hold on to the body of God. You can see things in the body of a priest— is that it? The folds and flap of all the black show parts of Him, and the inside of Him, and the gug of a place inside the Book. Smoke from the gob of brine burning on an animal is holy. Peter lifted his arms and prayed over a clump of dirt and a flag in the churchyard. He cut the skins and clutched them. There was a woman with a limp and a back hump.

74

She kissed him. Hands bent in the church—hands were bent into churches. They would take me to the church. The wood was thick. The wood had in it a black spot. There was a scratch in the pew. Mother kneeled. She would touch you with the water. His shawl once slipped from his shoulder. They were saying the name—what a spot soft of talk!—next to her, to the house, here I am.

I am all here alone.

One of the men there had hands like mine. She showed me. The picture was next to the pin. There was another one in another room. The pig had fat lips and a hat. Its tail was in a man's hand. The cup had a gold rim. A plump horse in the moss had a hoof high and a pup in its mouth. The headboard had a felt, a leaf, a red swirl, a banding—these clotted up, cluttered little loose sheets and the bed next. His hand got stopped in the snow. It is true!—there were tiny toy boats, a tiny boot, a tiny bell with a cross on top, a tiny man on his back, arms out, hands out, eyes open and white. There was a picture of a Jewish hand. I thought it was an elephant. The picture was next to the rack with the crow, the zebra, and the ducks. I had a chair made of maplewood. I had a chest made of tulipwood. You gathered the blankets crushed, there, all your things together. Men made a line. There was a black train. There was a little pig in a cage. The lawns were frozen. Everybody got home.

The boat sank, actually. Food spilled down their wrists—a skinny post and a rib. Dogs were in the hold. The family drowned. The mother's carcass was found on a log afire in America. Her head was found in the wood. Her hands were hanging from a tree. Here—somebody said she was a giant. But the boat was not found in the sand of Long Island Sound! They would take me to the lake. Chunks of snow once fell off the choof. We saw a dog walking: bugs covered it until it was black.

The grass in along the brin and under it was green— but also gray. The grass had a burnt spot, a damp spot, a cracked spot up along a row of something— heels, bees—and along the first root of the tree, and even up a bit the trunk of the tree—slivers of bark and soot, pulp on the spot where he was standing. Her hem was patted down. Little bugs crawled all around a branch, on salt of a sort, or soil, one of the points moist and tilted, the sharpest point into the flat, the matting, the house—salt or soil, web, ribbon, one little bug on all its legs, but dead, however. The little bugs crawled all around the branch and they all crawled up onto the branch—the little bugs were coming to the door! The boxes broke. Rocks, bulbs, mulch—fell. Mother shut the shutters. There was the flit, the turning of her fingers to the part in the plate. The rain ruined the day.

Oh, I will be old soon.

I look like a bone.

A black plank on the roof: we start there. Their windows had dark wood, a block, silver, and a flower box. Things would fall down! Ice fell off. They said the rall is toof. The roof is tall to be kept and to keep us next to the breast of God. The overhang hung. There were these panes, those pendills at the end. The firestack was built of brick. The chimney had a twig and a dug. The rails had heads at the tops. The cornice had at its corners slopes and chipped trim. Bronze on one ball of rubble had a hole and a point—shingles, slats around, trunks, the V, heaving wood. There was a broken part at angles—how? This is the way their window opened—always slowly.

The dormers and the storm and her old-fashioned drawers! We were all well. The porch ran along until the pull of the wall under the latticework. There were fat nubs of shrubbery, bulbs, muttonskin—if you stood away. A dog walked across. Its ribs you could see, and its head—up and down, up and down. I would walk with them in short pants across the street. How I wish I had a house like yours. We once watched a house burn down—and you could hear the bells from the street. There was a walk back past the dog in the middle, the baby carriage, the nipple, the flapping tuft—wrinkled—and past the dent in the black plank. It is an old sound and I think it will be gone. The house did not fall down around our ankles! These beams made his cheek.

There was a portrait in their room. His hand was touching his chest. She stood next to him. Her hand was touching his shoulder. At the wedding the men sat on this side of the room. The women danced with the women; the men danced with the men. The sheet was blue. The opened box was red. The rabbi was walking past. The girl was next to the door. Her family was standing. His father sat in the chair. The bimah was next to the ark; the ark was next to the light. No!—I do not know if it was in that order at all. All the lights long in a row—it can be black or the body itself. But why are they lines? Bugs, an arm—a cemetery, naturally. The trunks of the trees were peeled and thick. Father would take me to the synagogue. The skullcap dropped! Your hand was in the flap of the coat, walking back. The inside of a synagogue is meant as a showing of—what? Is it the gibbet? A document defiles the hands of a Hebrew man. There was the word *neck;* the word *gag;* the word *Jew.* I never prayed for him. Rope and curtain hung over it. The frame was made of maplewood. Well—the walls there were of a certain curious sort. Spikes and curved brush curved next to the bricks. I liked walking next to her. Here were her other things, these lutty things. There was no wind. There was a portrait in their room. There was black on the brittle spot of the wall, all the thin spots in the house. His . . . his, His and his! The body was right here. The opened box was red. The closed box was closed. She touched the arm. She gulped at air. She was at the top step, next to the bench with the nebbins and the painted mouths—the moths, the black nub, Mother coming in and out of the room.

Okay. The inside, the outside. There were streaks

on her skin. I wanted to sleep inside his belly! The sound at death is all the air leaving your body. Maybe, too, it is God's last breathing there. God did not live with us inside our house. God did not crouch in front of our house, breathing beneath the door, clutching at the shutters. Here were the parts of the house, shape and portico. Here was the crib; here was the tub. Here was the branch scraping your window. There were the silvery things—a little bowl, a little thimble, a little ball. These terrible things!—the pillow, the wooden butcher, the three wicks in the pickle box. They were pointing up, falling out, tumbling—fat from the top, on top of your hand. These were the apples from the summer. She cooked lunch. He cleaned with a cloth the knife he had used to carve the meat. There was a stoking rod. Fritter and a jug were on the floor. Father was handsome. Can you remember his coat? Her hat came from an ancestor. The fur pushed back. Yes—she shut her eyes. The legs of the chair had circles and pikes. There was a chipped spot, another chipped spot, so small, a corner, dirt. What, though, was cuffed and folded over? She sat down. The bedsheets and the headboard pressed. A cart was next to the wall. A hat was atop a box. There were wasps' nests in the house. There was another painting. Well—He did not die. He was holding on to a stick. Leaves and needles were in the road. A man covered his face with his hands.

Oh, Mother, I am so tired.

There was a hanging coat. A chair next to the door. An arm next to the pane. An empty box.

Everything ends there.

RAM FARM

HOOKS IN THE WALL

They took me to see some bulls in a barn. A man there held open a gate. A bull moved around a little in its kell. The bulls had black faces and white creases under the eyes. They picked up a stick and poked a bull in the face. The bull moved around a little and made a sound. It curled back its black eyeball. They waved for me. They pointed to a scar on the bull. They took me to another room in the barn. This one had hanging straps, harnesses. There were metal drums and tubs, smocks on a peg. A bull's head hung on the wall. There was an apple in its mouth. There was a gun on a slab. They picked up the gun and pointed the muzzle at their necks, shut their eyes. They fell on their backs on the ground. They made cracking sounds, breathing out of their mouths. There were some skins on bricks by a gate. They were piled and lumpy in the shape of a bull. They opened their eyes and smiled. They pointed to tall boys outside. Then they took me to see more bulls.

Lips, snout, stomach, hooves. Some hog tails are wet with little shoots that cut your hand. Some hogs frown when they are in pain. My father once made his face that way to show me. Yorkshires, Berkshires, Hampshires, Lambshires, spotted swine— these are kinds of hogs. These are names of hogs on the farm—Holy Roland, Roly Joe. It is good luck to use the name of a man who lived a long life. The way a hog grunts can make it seem the hog is saying your name. Lump jaw, hark jar, Bang's. Muscle and bone make up the feed. Almost everything is eaten. You can eat slices of the liver fried—with hot blackberry sauce and pear cream on the side. The brain can be boiled with vinegar and celery root. Add gingersnap sauce or rub with a lemon. Hold it under cold water, scrubbing it the way my father did—brushing in small circles with the thumb. Make a flour paste and use bell peppers. The bodies of hogs! I admired their size. I admired their strength. I thought that the pigs slept inside the hogs at night. You can touch the spot in the air right here where one once was.

THE WOMEN
IN THE WINDOW

The hogs come up this way, side by side, rubbly, bucking up their faces. They are happy! The hogs in the morning—past pigs, snouts into a sow, and hogs eating at the creep socket, and hogs through the creep slat. The hogs running—a hoof up this way, a kind of grin, a hoof up this way, a tusk, a flak of dirt. The hogs duck, bump, coming for us, their hair in sharp ends, their hips just hair and a crease. The hogs! The hogs come up to us this way, almost falling over, seeming almost to tiptoe, ready to line up tonight outside our house, lobbing rocks at the shingles, one by one, over their shoulders, fancily, without looking at what they want to hit.

RAM

The bark rake, the pig rack, the pigeon gill—I remember the barn. The barn was in the First Corner. They called the First Corner the Fist Corner. We watched a shot bull roll in the palm! A horse died right here, while eating off a boy's foot. Green lat had made the horse's face bleed and its belly black. A boy with no arms once bent over and trembled out his tongue to touch his toe—for one dollar. Somebody chased him away. The bark rake on the barn made one of the fingers a flap of wood—and were you afraid of all you could fall under all day the way I was? The fire, the broom, the father—claws and the tub through the ceiling the next time! The portrait on the wall of the father carrying the son, the son seeming to fall even in the portrait—in the house in the Second Corner. They called the Second Corner the Sick Corner—and the Bone or the Elbow or the Point. The mother was dead. They lifted me up to see. Our house was in the Third Corner. They called the Third Corner Schwartz. The house, the door, the rail—I remember the rusted window silver, the crusted shit by the sitz cow! They also called our corner the Shoulder—and the grass slope was the high, meat part of an arm. The cracks in the dirt were the veins. They called all of Ram Farm God's Arm.

My father brought up a dog before breakfast. He had the dog call up at the boys who were standing on the roof, cracking ice. It was so cold there in the morning! A man would squeeze on my hat and tug my ears and give me a cinnamon hook after lunch. My father once sat backward on a bicycle. I knew what the girl kneeled for. Look at the snow! The men would dig us out and sometimes a horse would come with us. My father sometimes stood on a rung of a gate and held his hands together to sing down at the pigs. One of the boys pinned back a pig's legs. I wore a sailor's blouse! A man used a bucket under the bull—cutting, pulling from the bull. One of the boys showed the trick in his hand—the brad, the penny, the thumb covered up. There were so many men there! At night a man would lift me by my arms and carry me up the steps. A boy would help me into the house. My father would shut the door.

III

ROUTE

Here is the building.
Well, the colonnade—the balcony.

The sculpture, one concedes, is chipped.

There is always mention of the drapery, furthermore, pertaining to the way it falls across the
shoulder—pertaining, indeed, to the sharpness of a
pleat.

The road bends.

Oh, and the square—the square is famous. There
is a tomb, you see, or a fountain—it is to this effect,
in any event. An inscription cites a great fever—
which accounts for the soldiers, it would seem.

The city was invaded on this day in 1680.

Common oaks grow outside the fortress—where,
evidently, a foreign woman, a countess, was executed: early in the morning, by hanging, the hem
of the gown a bit frayed, it should be explained, from
age.

The hat shop is open today, but the butcher shop

is closed. There are kiosks, too—one sells trinkets, another sells Stilton cheese.

There is an obelisk near the river.

A man mispronounces the name of the bridge—yes, and he blushes.

But the building—do you see the balcony there? And the little mark on the column? There is a flag. There is a broken pediment.

A woman stands at a gate.

One, of course, is easily lost.

An excursion.

The town hall is well known for its volutes, but the gentleman discusses, instead, a bust of Agrippa, which has been stolen, and the house's oriel window, through which, according to the story, Bismarck once saw a ghost. Marshal Turenne was killed in Sasbach, in fact, not Gernsbach, so, no, it will not be possible today to see the plot and the stele—though, happily, there is—if you will forgive the crude juxtaposition—a view from the keep: yes, look, such a remarkable hillock. He adverts to the wind in the castle's courtyard, which is solemn, and to the garden, which is formal, and to the servant who strangled the children on the grand staircase—

which leads, as you can now see, to the room of mirrors, where a woman is tidying her hair.

I bundled the letters. I kept the photograph—or I saved it, if you would prefer. The map was torn. The newspaper had been discarded.

It did begin to rain. I naturally felt a bit foolish. I held the rail. There were pots of flowers, passersby. Somebody pointed at a telamon.

I suppose the door was locked.

But the soldiers—let us return, if we may, to the soldiers. They died, you will remember. There is always mention of the bedclothes—and the bannister, the little birds, that pattern on the wall.

Oh, now the square, on the other hand—there are no pigeons, for instance, in the square. Here are the people, though. There is actually something of a crowd.

Other facts occur to one.

The hat shop is open today, but the butcher shop is closed. There are wrinkled curtains in the windows of the dance hall—which was built after the war. This house was once the residence of a general.

The bedroom faces the river.

A history indicates the manner in which the objects on the table were arranged—the ink blotter here, the stack of paper there—oh, and that he wore a herringbone coat the day he murdered his brother.

There is a handsome drawing of the pistol.

The hospital is the same hospital—and the benches, at least, do strike one as old. The park is austere, according to the diary—but green, merely, according to a letter—in which there are also references to anguish.

A small purchase is made.

The road, as we have already remarked, bends.

The building—well, come a bit closer. Now the ornamentation is distinct, certainly. Guilloche— torus. One considers a blemish at the center of the design. One considers the elevation of the capital.

The sculpture does not resemble the *Apollo Belvedere* or the *Cnidian Aphrodite*.

There is a flickering here, a glint.

But the balcony—you can see the balcony, of course. A woman opens the doors in the morning, at this hour. The balusters are urn-shaped—yet this fact, one imagines, claims very little.

A letter lists dates.

There follows a digression concerning a man who was poor, whose children were not well, whose wife—we should be plain—died. The man's screams were said to have been louder than the screams of a certain king—to whom we shall return.

The river floods on occasion.

The road is named for a countess, quite clearly, not a baroness, even if the latter title is the one indicated on the map—on which, furthermore, the legend is blurred. At any rate, now and then there are parades.

But the building—but there is apparently something amiss in the archway. And you will please pardon the little mark on the column—and the shadows on the steps.

The flag snaps about a moment.

A man walks across the lawn.

An engagement.

Well, a misadventure.

Monument, one is told, derives from the Latin root for *monster.*

The diary, however, does refer to a more ame⁻ hour—and there is, certainly, some shapeˡ the day. How one wants everything to be

95

stones along the road, the engraving. Is it clever to suspect the inscription? The wind? The manner in which the handkerchief is lifted into the air?

I suppose it was taken late in the day—or that there was something untoward about the light. Here, all the same, is the boulevard. There are automobiles, a signboard. A name is shown on a shop's awning.

The fellow is smiling. My wife is wearing a hat, a scarf, gloves.

The roof of the hotel is cut off.

But the window—but is there a woman at the window? The countinghouses, according to the diary, resemble Napoleon's hands—and there is some mention of an alley.

There are blind arcades and Lombard columns—and a square coping. King Leopold's skull, if we are to believe the story, is buried at the foot of the tower; the pavilion has a Baroque facade.

The frieze has carved faces.

The map indicates a fortress, a river, a dam. This ˙s named for a burgher—who once lived in this ˙use. This road is named for a margrave—
˙meal was haddock, stewed prunes, water-
˙opped gherkin.

The museum displays a madder-colored garment, a tunic.

How one does speculate about the clothing—and about the bed, naturally. There is, as you know, a purse; let us presume that the stationery is new.

A letter lists cities—and dragon's blood, ostrich plumes, a gizzard. There is a description of a lawn.

A man stands at the steps.

The sculpture is chipped.

The window, of course, is dark.

TURRET
The Square

The sun, in any case, and the walk: out in front, early, like this. Keep in mind the season. The tack, alas. Sacks of fruit, the manner of the soldiers. The captain, it is remarked, was an orphan. The chambermaid had asked forgiveness. The governess loses her hat in the wind. There are parcels: *Stoop. Pistol. Jaw. Pyx.* A medallion and a package of chocolate. Keep in mind the flies. The Jew, it is remarked, was handsome. The steward's tongue had been bored through. The quartermaster had escaped. There is little fuss over the doors, over the shutters. A child pulls a necklace from the widow's throat: out in front, early, like this.

The Fortress

Sacks of fruit, a pistol: inside. A bolt of cloth beneath the door? An embarkation of sorts. Outside: barrels and a shroud, a patch of crabgrass. There are sticks in the ditches, horses at the wall. Dogs athwart. The sun returns? These bats, in any case. Keep in mind the hour. The bell: the bells. Certainly the sweeping of the steps. Now: the brothers, one by one. You can hear them? A brick sits atop the scaffold's drop.

The Rooms

One, she said, or the other.

It seems the widow was a different matter.

There were prunes in a stockpot, pecans in a tin.

Simply the view, this time, and the wind—or the clouds and the quarter hour. Simply the beggar's-lice and the oak trees, the names of the towns.

She was so sorry.

It seems the boroughs were through.

The afternoon, the visit, the meal: a bit of mischief concerning a lock.

She tried, she said, to think of pleasant things.

Simply the roofs, after the usual manner—or in a certain light.

One, she said, or the other.

There was an ornament above a door.

The Fortress

Remains, of a sort: inside. Collected digits? For purposes of counting. Outside: dogs, barrels, ditches. Teeth are buried at the foot of the scaffold. Coins are buried at the foot of the cannon. Now: a soldier is thrown from a horse. At the great wall? It is greater, in any case. Ribbons: gone. Posts: gone. Ropes: gone. There are stones and wasps. Carts, of a sort, in the courtyard. Toppled? Overturned, if you please. A gown is buried at the foot of the gate.

The Square

s and ledges, in any case: the ridges of
verpots. The houses have brown shut

ters. The doors, it is remarked, resemble coffins. There are signboards: how nice. The suitor spills a bottle of wine. These roofs, the fruit market. The general eats ladyfingers off a white plate. There are parcels: *Beauty. Loom. Monstrance. Gullet.* A package of chocolate and a tin of pecans. There is a bit of mold on the bread. A row of tall windows, feathers, the ridges of dirt in the flowerpots. The chambermaid, it is remarked, had contrived to die. Pigeons move about. A carriage of nuns passes in the road.

BALUSTRADE

The woman removes her hat and gloves. The fellow sits on the ottoman.

The bowl is cracked. The vase, in truth, is not one of the gifts. The newspaper, from which a page has been torn away, reports upon a steamship lost at sea. The bureau stands next to the balcony doors.

There is a draft.

The woman touches the cuff of the woollen blanket. Milk curdles in the fellow's coffee.

Oranges sit in a bowl on the windowsill.

There is a view.

The fellow tells a story about the boulevard.

A soldier, who wore a uniform with brass buttons, stood before a house. The house was ablaze.

The soldier uttered a Latin word.

Consider this.

The barber brought flowers in the evening.

Next to the vase sits a package of chocolate. The earrings sit in the top drawer of the bureau. The newspaper, which the fellow slowly folds, reports upon a holiday supper in Dessau.

There was peach cobbler for dessert.

A child wore a ribbon at her throat.

The woman bathes. The fellow combs his hair.

It rains.

Consider the box of matchsticks—which the fellow drops. The newspaper, which the fellow sets atop the bureau, reports upon the grandeur of a certain opera.

The fellow undresses before a mirror.

There is a draft.

On a ledge sits a Latin grammar. The spine of it is green.

The fellow reads.

Amplector, amplecti, amplexus sum.

Lateo.

Morior.

The fellow remarks upon a flaw in the wood. The woman pours water into a tumbler.

Oranges sit in a bowl on the windowsill.

The steamship, on which had been served, every morning, shirred eggs with paprika, fresh herring, and sliced sausage, was lost at sea. The barber, who had loved the daughter, brought flowers in the evening.

The fellow describes his home.

The first room was blue. His aunt would wear a polka-dotted scarf. His brothers would cry in the night. His sisters would sit on the lawn and bunch their skirts.

There were chrysanthemums and birch trees.

There is a view.

Consider the river—which, the fellow says, is a pleasant color.

There was a Christmas pageant in the afternoon—and a great embarrassment.

The holiday supper, at which had been served split-pea soup and a rabbit fricassee, and at which the child had stained her dress and ribbon, ended rather late. The watch, which is old, and which is one of the gifts, sits next to the earrings.

It rains.

The windows fog over.

The newspaper, atop which the fellow sets a tumbler, reports upon a battle.

A town was taken.

The soldier, whose brother had died of scarlet fever, uttered a Latin word. The Latin grammar, the preface to which adverts to farce, has a green spine.

The fellow reads.

Opus est.

Anhelo.

Quid illo fiet?

A package of chocolate sits on a ledge. Oranges sit in a bowl on the windowsill.

The fellow tells a story about the boulevard. The woman folds back a corner of the woollen blanket.

The clove broke. Hence the penny's head. Hence the disquisition upon the nun's throat. The heirs, I understand, were fond of the dead furrow—all of it, here, the horses neglected, the knoll obscured. Surely the bonnet presumes the bones. In any case, the remains—the greater portion of them—had been preserved at the gallows house. Until Flitch Day, I believe. Imagine a tureen, or a colorful bowl, its lip—merely a moment of display.

But I do not wish to seem indiscreet.

The mourning turned, it was thought, in the horns of a new moon.

The Blackwall broke. The gimmal ring was a trifle? The bequest was small? There are—elsewhere, yes, in an older document—various phrases concerning the King's Evil, various phrases concerning a pestilence in France.

Cobwebs were apparent upon the ribs. The scarf—a grief, evidently—was discarded.

The trench puts it amply, I trust.

Why, a horse's hock, the coronet. Was it not thought bad luck to count coaches at a funeral? The chests were never locked at night. The seamstress did not touch the stitch to her mouth. Blood did not touch the shroud. In any case, a certain marriage fortune—some of it, perhaps the rest of it—had been lost. Not to mention the stones in front of the cottages. There were stems, nettles, thorns. Prettier errors. Poison for the vermin.

The belfry, I understand, had seemed a kind of blue ruin.

The cleaving was green? It is fine to imagine it this way, to imagine simply this—an array of points, like pistils, the coil feeble, all the baubles on the floor.

A bittern's claw had been pinned to the collar. A portrait had been made of the corpse.

Yet the name, the name—had they done away with it?

I stand abashed.

Surely the fire hunt was an afterthought. A feast for the ghosts, as the saying goes. Or something in commemoration. I cannot report that the porcelain chipped, that the glass cracked. The garret, however, collapsed.

The gimmal ring was copper.

A horse's poll? The stifle? The barrel will have to do. And as for the rattling of the coaches? There were—if you will indulge me—various customs for the children. The hair had been shorn. The regent brought devil's bit and a veil. The chests were buried. I am seized, indeed, by the passing bell, the notion of it—and by, moreover, this unhappy matter of the leaves and the needles.

There were dandelions near the cottages.

The bequest was great.

The carrick was brown—the fact of which, needless to say, does little to explain the servant's sobbing. In any case, circles of dust—upon velvet, upon wax—were thought to portend disease.

Cobwebs were apparent upon the spine. The stitch was a basting stitch.

The clove broke. May I note the bridle? The curl does seem apt, somehow. The nun's coin was kept. Doubtless, yes—a certain favorite object. The heirs, I understand, were fond of the bonnet, its knot, and of the henbane. But the sketches of the relics? Perhaps there was a resemblance of sorts. Why, simply a cut or a gown, this jot in the scenery—the wood white, like so, behind you.

He carries the urn from room to room. Never mind the scuffs, the various marks on the shelf. And the credence? The light is better elsewhere, you see. He examines the garment, just a ravel or a blotch—just the buttons, the color of the buttons—and these shapely pins and shapely catches. Hitches, actually. He examines the lists, most of the lists, or, at least, some of them, certain of them, largely the older ones, which had been fixed, once, in a bit of a bundle: think of the occasional—the odd—excursion, and of the visits, a tardy arrival or an early departure. Other arrangements were made? Their plot is prettier, you see. There was something for the aunt on the sisters' side? And for the brothers on the father's side? There was the matter of the niece's disease. The widower had jumped from a bridge. The son, it seems, had fallen beneath a train.

But before we lose our way.

———

Rings were contained in certain ancient urns. Pewter, though, according to the histories, was believed a rather gruesome intrusion. Etruscan urns resembled human forms. May I ask your opinion of the Saxon remains? The weight of the coins—this puzzles me. All the poor souls in the cold! Porcelain often signified the victim's pain. Horses—painted horses—often signified the family's misfortune. Many Roman versions address the processions.

The urn is without ornament. The windowsill is black. And the baggage? The satchel and the hatbox, to be precise. Given the visits, all the later visits, or, less bloodlessly, the last visit, which had been such a surprise, if not—to borrow their term—a success, the rest of it does sit a bit curiously, a bit wistfully. Yes, June or July, finally, or August—oh, or December, a day in December, merely an afternoon at the end of the year. Even the glass saddened them. Think of the bottles and the knives, a curtain turned back. Think of an error—a blunder—and these sounds in a house, a quilt at the foot of a bed.

The aunt was crestfallen. The brothers were the pallbearers.

The closet is locked.

Jews do not cremate their dead. Note, though, the holes made at the bottom of the casket. Should it not concern us to find cloth of a sort? A child's rent garment may be basted after thirty days. The *tzidduk ha'din* is always recited in full. The recessional—to abandon our example—invokes Zion and Jerusalem. Rain might be something of an exaggeration. The *reed* portion of the service is no longer performed.

Bruise is mistaken for *house* and for *hearse*—but this is probably for the best, given the hour of her departure—early, you will remember, so early—and given the manner—the humiliation—of his.

Gash is mistaken for *gift,* which accounts for the chifforobe, these remnants of the chifforobe—if not the credence, here, the wood of which—spruce? pine?—is, indeed, scarred.

Bone is mistaken for *frame* and for *burn*—though there is little reference to the blouses, to the scarves, to the gowns—or to, at any rate, the thread, which is green, terribly green, unwound a trifle, thus, and knotted.

There is—please allow a slight emendation—a trace, a simple trace of color at the urn's throat. Red, yes? The hatbox is brown. A valise sat at the aunt's knees. The doors of the train depot were thought endearing, while much prettier, perhaps, were the steeples and the hills—just the cut here, black, a tiny gap in the snow. The niece touched a thumb to a pleat in her skirt. Apparently the father had gone away. Oh, and the widower—the widower had jumped from a balcony, actually. Or from a window. The knives suffer modestly, you might say. The drapery falls drolly. The sound of the lock, I think, is not melancholy. No. Nor is this: the key, the keys—a clumsiness, simply enough.

Let the hitches suffice, and the handkerchief—which is gray, or, rather, not quite white.

The Slaughter of the Suitors adorns certain later urns. The quiver puts to rest those claims about swords, about state armor, about the carriage road. The sheath, though—this seems a more delicate matter. Bees explain the shade of the stain? The leaves cheer me. Many of the dates are curiously placed. Many of the chalice initials are reversed. I cannot find mention of the confessor.

He carries the urn from room to room. He examines the garment, just a ravel or a blotch—just the buttons, the color of the buttons—and this seam, a fine crease. Never mind the lists. Never mind the blinds—which, anyway, are drawn. The shelf is black. Indeed, think of burr walnut instead of birch. Or—to persist in this—think of blank elm instead of maple or beech or ash. The cane was pine. And the trunk? The satchel sat on the platform. The smoke was as dark as the train, blot by blot—now a picket, now the trim of a fence, and, darker still, these stakes beyond a hedgerow and a path, a steeple's crown. The room—the balcony and the window, to be precise—faced the lake. The widower had turned, first, to address his daughter. Think of hooks and a rail, the wallpaper's pattern. The brothers wrote out a name, over and again. The aunt wore a blue hat and a red—a maroon?—scarf. Yes, January or February, to the best of my memory, a Saturday at the beginning of February—or, more likely, a Sunday at the end of March.

Was there not a stumbling of sorts one morning?

The creaking of the door, you will agree, recalls a child's scream.

Caius Helvius Cinna was cremated at Diana. He had been mistaken for Lucius Cornelius Cinna—the praetor. Oh, walking quietly before a gate, I imagine, quietly placing an object upon an altar—all the lines white while our backs are turned. Cracked fasces often signified a sacrifice. Astragali often signified the family's despair. There had been a pin for a portrait, an ampulla for a vase. Yet shivers of glass—does such a presumption save us? The procession stopped at the father's monument.

Elements of the tea service. The bight and the drop-leaf table, at least. The cart, one should note, is thought unfortunate. There is something in the morning? There is a visit in the afternoon? The shape of the claw hammer, its face. Clutter enough. Oh, all one's foolishness about the rooms. The sachet card displays a woman on a balcony. The Berlinwork panel displays a slaughtered bird. Let us see. A man's name, as well. All one's foolishness about the lock, the bolt, the key. The color of this or that. We will discover a teaspoon upon the cupboard shelf? How unlikely. A creamer, perhaps. Speckled. Mottled, rather. Motes here and about. Oh, yes—something in the morning. A view, at least. Stones beneath the privet. Switches. Bees. This room had been the child's, you know. But how clumsy of one. Take the slant, the shape of the posts. The balcony is black. There is a curl of blood on the mask. And the rest is bright and dear? The teaspoons are overturned. The tarnished ones, if you please.

The crat and the cabriole, the lace napkins. And saucers, mind you. Oh, well. A saucer and a saucer. A visit in the afternoon, certainly. This room faces the road. See the knot, the dark knot. Perhaps it is a cardinal, actually. We have, at least, the way the woman waves. This and the dress. The needlepoint has left a mark on the wall, has it not? The chip in the rim of the teacup—this you might think a shade quaint. Whereas the hive? The privet in the wind? The switches are white. There is always a draft in the hallway. The windowsill, one should add, is scratched. The mirror seems another matter. A candlestick has rolled beneath a chair. True—one turns away. The teakettle and the place setting, the leaves of the drop-leaf table. And something in the evening? There are tiny initials on the knives.

SITUS

The lock was white. Its parts were not exquisite? Let me acknowledge the marks at the edges. The blot upon the ward, it was said, was the color of the lament. The pins were antique. As for the knives—well, I suppose I have been rather indelicate on this score.

The ax had been saved—dear me.

A certain narrative, as you know, depicts the visit—the corridor, the room, the rooms—and a leave-taking in the evening. The lamps—these— were lighted. It might be appropriate to note the sheet, moreover—despite the coins, the clatter of them, and despite the child.

The coil sat below the salt.

Knots, or figures such as these, adorned the bit— the slant quite bright, if we can envision it thus. The teeth—few, fewer—were brass.

For the Tudors and Stuarts, incidentally, a copper trill suggested a slaughter. Why, rats in the houses, black cattle—the very throat of the thought, you could say.

The lock was white, the shank crooked. The pins and the coil were silver. The arch was melancholy? To the contrary. Still, there was rot upon the crest. The escroll listed cities where the family had suffered. The escutcheon was scratched, naturally.

I am pleased—nay, delighted—by the tableau: a spot, just a spot, the key atop a box.

Embers might exaggerate the matter.

The narrative concludes rather oddly, in any case—alluding, as you will recall, to moonlight in an anteroom. They had waited, it would seem. The sheet shuddered and fell? Be that as it may. The hatchment cracked. The lamps were extinguished.

East.
There are goat's-tongues and cat's-paws in the water.

Silt chokes the bale.

The bow is the color of mazzards. Yes, to put it politely. Consider, in this vein, the wife's purse and the husband's necktie.

The starboard side: vultures "appropriate to the coast." Statements concerning the sun, the current, the cast of blue.

The port side: seagulls, naturally. Barrels. Chaise longues in disarray.

A stroll, one supposes—and a fall.

She faces aft. He turns.

A handsome staircase?

Miss Pike is cheerful in her distress.

The hall is dim. There are armchairs, empty armchairs, here, in a row.

The clock is not correct?

The wallpaper: green boxes and yellow knots, a marlinespike.

The lounge vestibule: a chandelier. Gizzards—to venture a guess. Marzipan and pecans. Capers. A glass of gin.

Pause, if you please, before the daughters.

Oh, but we have forgotten the piano, have we not? And the aquatint that hangs above the piano? Yes, consider the aquatint's caption—which alludes to a whipstaff, to a sailor staggering at a capstan, to a lantern oddly detailed. Perhaps there is a question concerning her preference, after all. Yet thieves under steam at the stern? A pistol? Maggots and weevils in the cheese? "A month's time"? Why, this would comprise something else entirely—as would, say, bodies on the rocks—to advert scenically, if inaccurately—and masts indistinct in the distance.

Luncheon.

In German black letter.

The mutton collops—to take an example—are served rare, with custard sauce, stuffed olives, and a raw onion.

Fillet of brill: for him.

The oxtongue and the devilled ham are ignored.

Chopped carrots. Diced, strictly speaking. Vegetable stew. Veal pie. Turnip puree.

Hearts of lettuce: for her.

The lemon meringue is preferred to the apricots—these, in the chipped dish—though the pits are thought pleasant enough.

The surnames are rendered in cursive.

Now, the manifest, the manifest—even if, all in all, the words are merely smudges—and even if most of the dates have been trimmed away, set aside, misplaced. No—mislaid is safer, you will agree. The grace lists dunnage and keeves. The inscriptions are unsigned. "For a grand couple." And: "To the charming honeymooners." The former suggests the knitting needles—the figure of which does contrive to a kind of prettiness, does it not? The latter suggests the bone china and the walking stick—and Mrs. Ash, who collapsed on the staircase.

A gray stateroom. Or: a wracked cabin.

Either will suffice.

And the rest of the afternoon is ruined?

Yes, actually.

There are garments of this sort and that. There is a jar of prunes beneath a porthole.

A Description of Ancient Navies: at bedside. Agrippa, one expects. The harpax. Swans and brine—stalks. Bones on the shoreline.

Brief Tales from Nautical Life: at bedside. Brief? Perhaps not, in fact. Tales? A treatise on maritime tragedies. A capsized schooner in place of a burnt rowboat. The helmsman's confession in place of the oarsman's rue.

The bookmarks are black.

The purse is brown, its buckle undone. The necktie is red—blood red, if you like. And as for our speculation upon the hat? Simply the buttons of the coat, the furrows, the pulls—or, at least, these spots in the wool. The trousers are striped and creased. The shoes have cracked heels. Is there not, as well, a hemmed—a mended—dress? The pocket watch has a decorative clasp, a severe face. There is a bit of grime about a hinge. An error accounts for the billfold, its color, and for the color of the trunk—and for, indeed, the hatbox—which—on a pier? in a harbor?—was lost.

———

Promenade deck.

A man touches her arm. She—how to put it?—she does not recoil. The drop dwindles in a neap tide. Think of a keelhaul—or of something akin to this. The anchor's hex, the throat of it, makes the matter plain. Or plainer, at any rate. The wake: like "pommel stiles." Consider the length of the hold, the bloat above the shoals. There are certain slashes and chimes. Statements concerning birds, the hour, the phase of the moon.

Now, if the shadows do, in fact, achieve the shape of a gallows tree, then what is one to conclude of the "gleaming" fissures in the wall? And if the planks' veins are stained—scarred, more likely—even a trifle, and if there is, as it were, a stitch in the skow—a rope, a rope—then what is one to conclude of the "anguished" lines? Of the "mournful" dashing?

But to step back a moment.

The badge records the loss of the *Saint George.* Lord Nelson's bullet, you should know, had been encased, with the corpse pennies, in a platinum locket. Lord Howard sat at table with peaches and a bundle of twine. He turned, if you wish, this way. The hitch had a black mouth. The mullet had a comely jaw, a gnawed gill. There was a pewter coffer atop the commode. As for the *Ariel*—well, the *Ariel* was destroyed by fire. The *Lady Anne,* which was destroyed by cannon shot, is often mistaken for the *Lady Jane*— which vanished in a storm.

Boat deck.

He fusses here rather grimly, rather gravely. Miss Lane is thought forlorn. And the daughters? Think of the flag, its staff—or of the bonnets and the snull on the bridge. But crowns? Dirge-knots in the fog? How presumptuous of one. There is a disturbance on the lee side, at any rate. Consider the steam—and the ladder, which is crooked, here, and wet. The drop dwindles in a neap tide. There are certain slashes and chimes. The breeze is agreeable—if colder now, much colder.

Shall we exclude the starlight? What little there is, after all. The king is not quite right. Nor is the cross. The keening is our misfortune. Oh, a chained body in the North, simply enough—and the children, drawn and quartered. Is it as black as all that? Saturn—in a calm—is the color of a wounded barrow. So they say. Berenice's hair is more easily observed. When the horns of the moon turn—in autumn, in the rain—Aries resembles an urn.

Dinner.

In copperplate.

The silver hake is served with anchovies, giblet dressing, sweet gherkins, and boiled potatoes. The cutthroat is served with beetroot.

The spine is something of a surprise.

Mincemeat pie: for her.

Dwarf perch or herring—a sprat, one takes it. Yes, and the remnants of the whelks: for him.

Split peas and bitter almonds. Consommé andaloux. Waldorf salad. Queen fritters. Portuguese macaroons.

There now—a proper list.

The surnames are rendered in cursive.

It is bad luck to save the knives for last, one hastens to add. Notice the rotundity of certain utterances. "Please help him." Or: "She'll not go." Or: "I can say nothing more." Oh, as the evening proceeds. As objects drop from the purse. Ribbon of some kind—red ribbon. And: a tarnished spoon. The former recalls the crack in the spool's lip—if not the claws,

125

the rabblement of moths—if not the rattling in the legs of an armchair. The latter recalls the teakettle's copper bottom—and apples altogether too brown, the flesh of them, the skin.

Her lament—brief or otherwise. His maudlin little notion.

Just so.

Mr. Grove draws back in fear.

The veranda: a trellis and a pair of gloves. Squares of light on the floor.

The ballroom: a posy and a vase. This arrangement of tables to our right.

There are sailor's-eyes in pots along the wall.

"Mother in the Snow": quaintly. For voices.

"Sorrow in My Heart": for brass instruments. In, it seems, three parts. Haltingly? With a desultory chorus? At long last?

The shanks are another oversight, obviously—as are the blood pudding and the offal. One imagines—perhaps foolishly—a woman addressing herself to her hands. The color of the beading is unclear. Yes, simply the baize before the flukes, after all. Simply the shad before the agraffe. The dress hooks have not made a favorable impression—though the dent is thought a touching defect. And the manifest, in our absence, has curled at the corners? Or torn? And fallen from a shelf? The year is engraved upon a bronze plate.

She blanches. He blushes.

Mr. Parson slips at the trup.

The lounge vestibule: trenchers. Gristle and caul, a ewer, carved oak. There is a pattern on the ceiling.

The mirror has a gilt frame.

The wallpaper: green boxes and four o'clocks, a watchtower.

The daughters stand at a door.

What is here, this way, behind the posts?

One wishes for something serene, you see—or for, at least, a view of the staircase and the landing, the lamps at the end of the hall.

East, indeed.

There are goat's-tongues and cat's-paws in the water.

The port side: a gaggle of this or that. A cudgel atop a crate. Barrels. Statements concerning waves, ballast, the neck of the coast.

Fixing the hour, as it were.

The starboard side: clouds at the trow. Foghorns, surely. Surely a deck light's reflection. Letters written out across a flap's bite.

Here is the husband—but where is the wife?

There is a bend in the stern rail.

The breeze ceases.

THE STAVES

The effigy was always burned rather gaily apparently. The band would play in the road. The ribbons and the banners, I suppose, would hang from the posts. There are, in passages in Saint Thomas, his hair and the bier, for instance—thus the pomp, thus the haw. In Saint Matthew—daffodils, the dot on the body, the question of the widow, a quaint explanation of the cloaks. In Saint Philip—a procession in Galilee, which is apropos, is it not?—though a bit curious, too, actually, given how, according to Saint Peter at least, the bones were arranged to form a cross. I hate to think of grave things—though it occurs to me that I have already confused various of the phrases, that I have perhaps mistaken one verse for another, that there is a moment at the conclusion of a sermon wherein an array of serpents appears in a potter's field, the location of the sun invoked for this reason or that, and he is buried.

Observe, then, reader—we are safe here. Do you

see? The Pharisees were whipped and stoned—while, for instance, women called to the goats. The day, of course, ended, which is pretty for us—save the image, it seems to me, of the open gate—save the fact, obviously, of the leeches upon the priests' feet. It gives me a fright—though the pommée and the bleat are, after all, so dire, are they not? The ridge apparent in the wood somehow reminds me, however, of that Dürer painting—the grand red stripe at the edge, the unfortunate boys, the tiny hat for naught. But please forgive me; I will try to make this quite clear. He was shaking so. He hid (as such). He spoke (possibly). The Gospels indicate he dropped the silver coins in the temple, that he hanged himself in Qumran. Or, on the other hand, no—indeed, certainly not, as he actually rode in an animal cart through a pass, as he actually fell in a field in Emmaus.

Thus—Maundy Thursday.

Thus—Good Friday.

The effigy was always marked, first of all, about the neck—mud, probably, or soot, albeit only a smudge, really, as per a certain parable—which is an oddly charming point, I think. But are we to believe such things, finally? That Saint Francis's alb was boiled in a stew at a priory in Portugal? That a

Sadducee's bowl contains a lock (as they say) of the hair? That the straw represents the purse? That the powder represents the ashes? Behold, in other words, the body. There is an engraving (fourteenth-century, if I remember correctly—English, maybe) that displays a figure in, if you will, his eternal torment—and so a neat column of flames and a loop of beehives, for instance, are introduced in the foreground. There is one with horses, too—in the corner, in the bramble, in gallop, manes to and fro, it would seem, the horses facing one another, or, again, no—one is looking away. I love the olive trees (there is a sort of stateliness, is there not?)—beneath which, moreover, are lines of arrows and ovals that, arranged thus, indicate, why, not very much at all—as far as I can see, anyway. The inscription mentions how he was brought to the tomb—days in the wilderness, to begin with; the row of camels in the road; the hair cut off, the thumbs cut off, the tongue cut out.

There is a Spanish word for his footsteps.

The monks would walk in the morning, you know. The effigy was always marked elsewhere, also, on Holy Saturday, unless I have not understood the story properly—the wrists and the ankles, naturally; the reddish streak about the lips, of course. There are older stories—the sexton stood in the belfry; the cassock was drawn to the hip; the church cat was fixed; the puppet was cinched and then dipped in tar (by the vicar). How it wounds me, this notion—though I wonder if they were saved, on the other hand, something concerning Mary's hair in May and the women walking with baskets to market—hew, I imagine, crocks, a home—so merry, so merry. But in fact—the goats were all gone, higgledy-piggledy, down the hill, far away; and he appears, actually, in none of the drawings, anyway, except the one in Saint Bartholomew's book—gargoyles for the birthday, and blots, only, for the wife on Saint Agnes's Eve—the skulls and the like, even the smoke next to the lists of the names—whereas she died, as you know, oh, somewhat less well.

But to continue. I have never known quite why the bits of wax were placed here and there, near the altar, in the pew, for the Mass—and, either way, indeed, how does this explain the lovely ivy on the walls of the abbey? Saint Bathildes ate cabbage for lunch every day—with the prelate, who was ill. Saint Jerome sat in his cell—the engraving shows this (and, too, candlesticks and a statue of Saint

A NOTE ON THE TYPE

This book is set in Spectrum, the last of
three Monotype typefaces designed by the
distinguished Dutch typographer Jan
van Krimpen (1892–1958), originally commissioned from him in 1941 by the publishing house Het Spectrum of Utrecht.
Spectrum surpasses van Krimpen's other
faces in both the elegance and versatility
of the letter forms but shares with Lutetia
and Romulus many qualities characteristic of van Krimpen's designs—fine proportions, sharp cut, and generous counters.

Composed by ComCom,
Allentown, Pennsylvania

Printed and bound by Quebecor Printing,
Fairfield, Pennsylvania

Designed by Misha Beletsky

Christopher). Saint Anthony looked away—this is in one or another of the lives. A cross was there by chance, just the hasps, or a shadow, a wisp of something on his hand, they say, the moment before his death—though they are uncertain on the subject of the sunlight—though they are uncertain as to the figure of the attendant, about whom they include a pun, as it happens. The body was perfumed and costumed, and the face was hidden—though maybe this is melancholy to consider.

In any event.

I like to think of the ceremony—hoods, filigree, the folds in the drapery, you see, the breeze in the trees in the arbor. Well, this sort of moment, yes— but I am wrong, of course. A cat was once thrown from the tower on Easter Sunday—and Saint Babylas refers to buzzards and to a spot of dirt in Spain. The effigy was always brought to the church steps noon, certainly. I have always imagined a great lowing of the cloak in the wind—though t' probably silly of me, is it not? The ministrant ring the bells. The band would march b forth in the road. The ladder, I take it, wo

Christopher). Saint Anthony looked away—this is in one or another of the lives. A cross was there by chance, just the hasps, or a shadow, a wisp of something on his hand, they say, the moment before his death—though they are uncertain on the subject of the sunlight—though they are uncertain as to the figure of the attendant, about whom they include a pun, as it happens. The body was perfumed and costumed, and the face was hidden—though maybe this is melancholy to consider.

In any event.

I like to think of the ceremony—hoods, filigree, the folds in the drapery, you see, the breeze in the trees in the arbor. Well, this sort of moment, yes—but I am wrong, of course. A cat was once thrown from the tower on Easter Sunday—and Saint Babylas refers to buzzards and to a spot of dirt in Spain. The effigy was always brought to the church steps at noon, certainly. I have always imagined a great billowing of the cloak in the wind—though this is probably silly of me, is it not? The ministrant would ring the bells. The band would march back and forth in the road. The ladder, I take it, would creak.

A NOTE ON THE TYPE

This book is set in Spectrum, the last of three Monotype typefaces designed by the distinguished Dutch typographer Jan van Krimpen (1892–1958), originally commissioned from him in 1941 by the publishing house Het Spectrum of Utrecht. Spectrum surpasses van Krimpen's other faces in both the elegance and versatility of the letter forms but shares with Lutetia and Romulus many qualities characteristic of van Krimpen's designs—fine proportions, sharp cut, and generous counters.

Composed by ComCom,
Allentown, Pennsylvania

Printed and bound by Quebecor Printing,
Fairfield, Pennsylvania

Designed by Misha Beletsky